IZZY IS A MOUNTAIN GIRL. SHE LIVES ON TOP OF THE WORLD. TODAY'S THE BIG DAY! HERE COMES THE BUS...

For Mrs. Lipscomb, my first-grade teacher

Special thanks to Kim Denkers, Elaine Berns, and the Maple and Oak preschool classes,
The Colby School, Park City, Utah

Reinforced binding

First Edition

Printed in Singapore

3 5 7 9 10 8 6 4 2

Library of Congress Cataloging-in-Publication Data on file.

ISBN-13: 978-0-7868-3896-7

ISBN-10: 0-7868-3896-5

Visit www.hyperionbooksforchildren.com

Additional art by Cris Kowanko, Isabella Canada, and Josephine and Isabel Neubecker.

Wow! School! was drawn in india ink with a brush, on Arches watercolor paper.
The color was done on a Macintosh computer with a mouse!

WOW! SCHOOL!

by ROBERT NEUBECKER

HYPERION BOOKS FOR CHILDREN
New York